T0107296

"Adam and Eve…
Their Love Story Continues"

"Adam and Eve…
Their Love Story Continues"

A story by Marsha Green

iUniverse, Inc.
New York   Bloomington

Adam and Eve... Their Love Story Continues

iUniverse books may be ordered through booksellers or by contacting:

iUniverse
1663 Liberty Drive
Bloomington, IN 47403
www.iuniverse.com
1-800-Authors (1-800-288-4677)

Because of the dynamic nature of the Internet, any Web addresses or links contained in this book may have changed since publication and may no longer be valid. The views expressed in this work are solely those of the author and do not necessarily reflect the views of the publisher, and the publisher hereby disclaims any responsibility for them.

ISBN: 978-1-4401-2726-7 (pbk)
ISBN: 978-1-4401-2727-4 (ebk)

Printed in the United States of America

iUniverse rev. date: 3/30/2009

To the most beautiful boy in my world - My 20 year old son, Grant,-Thanks for proofreading my book!

To my significant other, Greg, - Thanks for editing my story and for all of your support through the publication process.

And to my amazing English Setters, Jet and Jazz, who stayed close by while I wrote this novel.

CHAPTER 1

Jay Reed was considered "hot property" by all the studios in Hollywood. After landing a starring role in "Exit Line", his first movie, his fame skyrocketed and he became what critics called an "overnight success". His face was featured in People magazine as the "sexiest man alive". He also did a spread in Playgirl with a picture of him coming out of a pool in a thong talking about his latest movie "The Red Bull" coming out in six months. From then on his life consisted of highballs, cigarettes, fast cars, and loose women. There were endless parties and one night stands with some of the most beautiful girls in Hollywood. Whenever he recalled the night before, the memory was usually a blur of a pretty face and a decent body. He dated models, actresses, and production assistants on the set.

He was a compulsive gambler and frequented the casinos in Las Vegas. Whenever he traveled to Las Vegas, he could be found at the craps table. Each trip to Vegas was always preceded by a newspaper clipping by his publicist who announced he was headed there. He would find a string of girls waiting for him outside the casino. "There're my lucky ladies!" he would say and would give each one of them a kiss and a hug.

When Reed was a baby his father laid a baseball signed by Ernie Banks and wooden bat in his crib. "Don't you think you could have started with a plastic bat and wiffle ball?" his mother had said to his father. "Margie, someday he'll be a baseball player for the Cubs." His mother merely rolled her eyes.

In high school Jay Reed had the notoriety as an "all around jock". He not only was on the baseball team playing shortstop, remembering the many times he had played pitch and catch with his father, but he also played basketball. He dated the class president, several cheerleaders off and on, was homecoming king, and wrote a sports column for the school paper. He stumbled into a drama degree from Madison College quite by accident. He had accompanied a friend to acting class and volunteered to do a scene. He played the role of an FBI agent in confrontation with a criminal. He had done so well the teacher had asked him to come back. The next semester he enrolled in Drama One. From then on he continued to play baseball, but instead of trying out for the major leagues, he chose acting.

Following graduation he packed his bags, sold his furniture, and left his hometown of Chicago for Hollywood. It was a blow to his self esteem when his father said "An actor! You'll never get in the front door!" But Reed proved his father wrong. After "Exit Line" made him 20 million dollars,he bought his parents a 2 million dollar house on the outskirts of Chicago.

CHAPTER 2

When Jay Reed first arrived in Hollywood, he parked cars at an exclusive restaurant. Bess Morris, an agent, spotting him and noticing his good looks, gave him her business card and said to "look her up". He called her office the very next day and got an appointment at nine am to see her the following day. He was relaxed, and when interviewed by her, assumed a laid back demeanor. She heard about his degree in drama and listened intently to him telling her about his experiences in college playing Hamlet, Woody Allen's "Play it Again Sam", and Alfred Hitchcock's "Rear Window".

At the end of the meeting, she handed him a card with the name Tex Myers on it along with a phone number. He was to call him and get an audition to be in a tooth paste commercial. He was expecting to audition for a part in a movie and was highly disappointed. He called Myers anyway and found out the audition was the next day.

He arrived at the Myers Production Studio to find an

office full of beautiful young men. He noticed one man was paging through a magazine; another simply staring at the wall; another tapping his toes and fingers; and another writing in a notebook.

Forty-five minutes later he was called into Myer's office. His secretary, a skinny 40ish woman dressed in black with a severe overbite was sitting beside him. Myer, a baldheaded man with a cigar in his left hand said "So you want to be in show business?" Reed replied "That's been my goal". "Well," he said "Show me what you've got", Myers said handing him a script.

Reed looked it over briefly and began. His husky voice resounded off the walls in the room.

"Good" Myers said. "Take a seat in the outer office," he instructed. Thirty minutes and two other interviews passed. Then Myer's secretary motioned for him to reenter the office. He got the role of announcing in a 60 second commercial how he got the whitest teeth in Hollywood. Then he went back to parking cars. Two months later he got a call from Bess Morris Agency to audition for a starring role in "Exit Line", and the rest was history. That was 3 years ago and now he was a star.

CHAPTER 3

Jay Reed's motto concerning women was "There's a girl for every occasion and for every occasion a beautiful girl". He was engaged once to a beautiful young actress, but never got past the bachelor party. When his guy friends took him bar hopping to celebrate the engagement, he ended up taking a waitress home. He never considered himself a sucker for women, but merely a survivor.

He had witnessed several of his friends falling for someone and then trapped in a mediocre marriage after the seven year itch set in. He vowed that would not be his fate and considered that fate had been kind to him in the area of the opposite sex.

He always made the Inquirer with his rough house antics. While on a break from the movie "You Can't Catch Me", he had sprained his ankle falling off a bar in a restaurant. He had been drinking and was dancing on the bar with a stripper. That incident cost the studio thousands of dollars having to postpone the film until his ankle healed.

He eventually hired 2 bodyguards he nicknamed Mutt and Jeff after a psychotic fan broke into his house. She began by writing him love letters mailed to the studio. The next incident alarmed him when she acquired a fake ID and got onto the set posing as a production assistant. The authorities were called and merely gave her a warning much to Jay's dismay.

Her next stint occurred the following week when she had broken into his home and ransacked the place. He walked in, saw the mess, and discovered her on his living room couch attired in a g-string and high heels. He called the police, had her arrested, and pressed charges that sent her to jail. His bodyguards didn't accompany him everywhere, but for the most part did, keeping a safe distance behind him.

Jay Reed always felt safe; however, he was being watched. No one, including his bodyguards could have known.

CHAPTER 4

Drake Roberson was a self-made billionaire. He was as cunning as a snake lying in wait to strike his next victim. In business deals he was as shrewd as a fox and barbaric as a cannibal. Devious was his middle name. By the mere age of forty he had built an empire.

Ten years ago he started out with $2500 dollars and invested it in residential real estate. He began buying nearly condemned houses; repaired them, and sold them for a profit. He later took his assets and began buying commercial property. He was as wicked as a cat cornering a mouse and sly as a lion stalking its prey in his deals. At forty, the name Roberson was well respected by the higher class of people in America.

His business deals were often corrupt but he always came out smelling like a rose. Similar to a lizard catching an insect with its tongue, he was quick to walk away from a deal with the better half of the profit. Roberson owned Star Line Casinos in New York, Chicago, and Las Vegas. He competed with another billionaire's casinos and was just as big. Roberson's slot machine players set the record in payouts making him the most successful casino owner in the state of Nevada.

Seven years ago he bought a fast food fried chicken franchise. His low cost lunch boxes boasted the best "Lip-Smacking Chicken" on the market and soon was sold throughout America and competed with General Lee's Fried Chicken Company throughout the U.S. Later he acquired a hamburger chain and named it Drake's Burger Deluxe which featured ten different sandwich toppings. He soon outsold one of the world's largest Burger chains nationally.

He became an icon, then, a living legend, but the buck didn't stop there. He bought hotels in several major cities and turned them into "Roberson's Sleep Inn". He still wasn't satisfied with his ventures and soon invested in factories in China that build household appliances; vacuums, toasters, coffeemakers. He undercut the price of those items and was the top competitor with every small appliance manufacturer in the country. His headquarters were in Chicago with other offices in New York. He owned a major hotel in Los Angeles and used the top floor for business dealings while he was in California.

At the age of twenty-five he married Nancy Waters whose father was a tycoon in the oil business. Drake Roberson figured it was more a business venture than a marital union. Following the marriage he invested heavily in stocks with National Oil and owned at least one million shares in the company. He was photographed frequently in public and there was always a pretty blonde or brunette by his side. Nancy soon learned her place was at home. She began drinking heavily after she realized her husband was a conniver, first rate horse's ass, and only married her for her father's money.

Drake Roberson never lost a bet, a deal, and never stuck his neck out for anything. He was a mastermind and had the world at his beck and call.

CHAPTER 5

Jay Reed was relaxing alone at home one night. At 8pm he was on his third highball and was lying on the family room couch with a fire blazing and the stereo on full blast. He sang out loud and off key to Mambo #5. The song could have been written for him, he thought, and laughed softly to himself.

By 9pm he was feeling a good buzz from the liquor and nodded off to sleep. He awoke an hour later by a noise he couldn't define. The stereo had stopped and the house was quiet again. His body was numb from the booze and he felt very woozy. Just then Mutt, his bodyguard, walked into the living room and said "Need help to get to the sack?"

"I'll get some z-z-z s here".

"Alright, I'm hitting the hay" Mutt said and retreated to his bedroom upstairs.

"Night" Jay called out, but his bodyguard had already gone.

The house was too quiet and he staggered to the

stereo. He flipped out Mambo#5 and put in a jazz cd. He was alone tonight, but didn't feel alone. There were usually two nights out of the week he crashed like this. He lay back down on the couch and drifted to sleep.

At 3am he was again startled by a noise in the house. "Shit" he said out loud. "What the hell is going on?" Then in his mind he saw the name "Adam". Then he heard a whisper... "Pssst - Adam". His eyes crossed for a second and he thought to himself…I'm dreaming…wake up.

He said out loud again "Jesus Christ"

"Jesus isn't here, Jay" another thought in words entered his mind.

I've just had too much to drink he thought. Better lay off the liquor, I'm dreaming awake! He shook his head, closed his eyes, and blinked twice.

"Adam" the whisper of a voice said again.

"What the hell" he said. I'm hearing things now, next I'll see sheep jumping fences or pink elephants and they'll put me in a detox unit to dry out.

"You're shitfaced", then he heard a low chuckle. He stood up somewhat awkwardly and grabbed the arm of the couch to keep from falling. "Later" the voice said. He stood up stupidly, then fell on his stomach to the floor and went fast asleep.

At 1pm, Jay awakened slowly and was blinded by the sunlight coming into the windows. He put his hand to his eyes. "Slept if off, huh?" the voice said again. "Drink some tomato juice, take two aspirins, and call your doctor".

Jay sat up and a note fell from his lap. The words were blurry, but he recognized his bodyguard's handwriting. "Went out for some grub" the note said.

"Let's get down to brass-tacks" the voice said. "W-who are you?" he asked out loud. "I'm the tooth fairy, who else. I'm God" the voice answered.

Recalling the voice from the night before he then asked "Who's Adam?" "You are Adam, and I'm Tinkerbell." "Where're Peter Pan and Captain Hook?" Jay muttered. "Smartass--a comedian is in my midst. Save it for the women." "Ok, ok" Jay replied. "Ugh" he said putting his hand over his forehead. "Hung over; you're a candidate for a Bayer commercial." "I could down a bottle right about now" Jay replied.

I'm dreaming he thought. "You're awake" the voice said in answer to his thought. "What's happening here?" he said out loud again. "Alright, movie star, let's get down to business" the voice said in a deep resounding tone. "You're Adam; remember the book of Genesis?" "Clearly" he replied and added "My mother put me in Sunday School for the first ten years of my life."

"Excellent" the voice said, then continued, "You are a 3,000 year old soul and your beginning was in the Garden of Eden as Adam. You were separated at death from Eve."

I'll play along with this, Jay thought. "Where's Eve?" he said.

"Somewhere on Earth" the voice replied.

"That narrows it down" Jay replied. "Smart mouth" the voice replied again.

Usually alcoholics have hallucinations of insects crawling on the walls, but I talk to God he thought. Playing along again he asked "I'm Adam huh? Why didn't you give me a last name?"

"Smart aleck, you didn't need a last name then."

Nowadays everyone needs a social security number, driver's license, and cell phone. A pause then the voice continued "Let's give it a rest and continue on better terms tomorrow. I'll walk you through it later on".

"Later" Jay muttered.

CHAPTER 6

Drake Roberson was a tyrant among his followers and demanded fierce loyalty from them. His right hand man was an individual named One Eye Jack. He was baldheaded and with a gold earring in his left ear and wore an eye patch on his right eye. Four years ago he lost his eye in a bar room brawl when he was stabbed in the eye with a fork. Three days later the man who stabbed him was fished out of the bottom of the Blue River with concrete blocks attached to his feet. There were witnesses to the incident in the bar, but no one stepped forward; being afraid of One Eye Jack's wrath.

In court Jon Peters, Roberson's high priced attorney, created an alibi for him saying he was at a restaurant, "The White Sheep", with friends. Peters persuaded a waitress to testify that One Eye Jack was at the restaurant at the time of death of the man. He was off the hook. One Eyed Jack's main job in Roberson's operation was as a "hit man". He carried a silencer illegally on his gun and "offed" men who jeopardized business dealings where

Roberson was attempting to acquire million of dollars with a company. These murders usually occurred with private-enterprise entrepreneurs.

Besides One Eye Jack, Roberson had another sidekick named Dr. Fingers. He stood 6 feet, 4 inches tall, had an extremely high forehead, a hawk-like nose, and a severe underbite. His face was grotesque and drew looks from anyone passing by him in public. The fingers on his left hand were missing. They were cut off 5 years ago by a machine in one of Roberson's factories he was working in. Dr. Fingers was then named by Drake Roberson after the incident. Proving to be a loyal follower, Roberson adopted the hideous looking man and made him his sidekick. Dr. Fingers usually accompanied Roberson as a bodyguard. He began working out with weights shortly after being assigned to the team and developed a massive body. Despite his large frame, he was extremely lithe. Aside from weight lifting, Dr. Fingers was a black belt in karate and taught classes in it to Roberson's many followers.

Roberson's third sidekick was a midget he called "Little Bit". He was in a traveling circus in Chicago three years ago and performed tricks with dogs in front of Roberson after hearing he was among the crowd of people there. Roberson laughed heartily as the midget danced around the dogs, making them jump through hoops and stand on their back legs. After the show Roberson sent a runner to find the little man and present to him a job with his operation. The midget was astounded and readily accepted the offer. That was 3 years ago and during the course of those years Little Bit's main duty was planting wiring devices in the hotel rooms of men Roberson was to do business deals with. Little Bit would listen, dictate the unsuspecting men's conversations, and turn in reports to Roberson.

Roberson's operations were intricate and well organized. His attorney, Jon Peters, rescued many jailers in courtrooms wanted for car theft, dealing in drugs, and even murder. Peters was shrewd and hadn't lost a case in court yet. Prisons were another source where Peters found followers for Roberson who employed top rate racketeers and con men.

Roberson also found followers high in government, sometimes even using blackmail to get them. They were involved in white collar crimes like extortion or embezzlement of large companies such as R.J. Reynolds or Phillip Morris. Roberson was also in the prostitution business. He had approximately one hundred pimps on staff throughout the United States. Drake Roberson was vicious, immoral, and corrupt.

CHAPTER 7

God returned the following day to Jay.

GOD: "Its time you know about what happened in Eden" he said in a deep, resounding voice.

JAY: "Alright, already; shoot".

GOD: "You're familiar with Genesis."

JAY: "Yes."

GOD: "That wasn't a question, it was a statement. I know all about you. I can tell you everything about yourself, even those things you've lost in your memory bank. I can also tell you everything about anybody you've ever met."

JAY: "Alright, I'm all ears."

God began to tell the story of what happened behind the scenes in the Garden of Eden.

GOD: 'There was a presence in Eden that wasn't mentioned in Genesis. It was Mother Nature. She created the animals.'

JAY: 'You mean you didn't make the animals?'

GOD: 'I made the heavens and the earth (his voice

rising), the night and day, the stars, and planted Eden. Not to mention the 10 commandments with Moses and bringing Jesus Christ back to life! Don't you think I did enough?'

JAY: "Ok, Ok. He put his hand up. "I'm with you, please go on."

GOD: "Besides, Mother Nature didn't want the publicity."

Jay laughed.

GOD: "She wanted to remain anonymous. You've heard of the Big Bang theory"

JAY: "Affirmative, in Science class."

GOD: "Yes. A big blast of molecules and atoms occurred and from this Mother Nature was created. Not in human form. She is a mind that is mobile by a force of air. She is the force of nature. All of her animals could procreate their own species, but what she witnessed in Eden was a very passionate love scene between you and Eve. She became extremely jealous and was envious of the relationship between you and Eve. She was a very powerful force back then but also a spiteful, vindictive, bitter force."

GOD: "She was instrumental in getting the Devil to trick Eve into eating the apple of the Tree of Good and Evil. After Eve bit the apple, the Fall of Man occurred and you and Eve were cast out of Paradise. Mother Nature was delighted by the outcome, but wasn't completely satisfied. She wanted to separate the two of you forever. Mother Nature created a "death force"; another mind concept which under her direction put Eve at one end of the Earth following her death and you on the opposite end of the Earth."

JAY: "But how could she get away with that?"

GOD: "Because I was of the opinion that Fate would play a hand in this and guide the two of you back together. You've been apart from Eve for 25 lifetimes now and during that time you never got anywhere close to finding her. Shall I go on?"

Jay nodded his head. He was dumbfounded.

GOD: "Your souls will circle Earth in perpetual motion and return at death again and again until you find her."

ADAM: "What happens when I find her?"

GOD: "Mother Nature goes away forever and you and Eve will then go to Heaven together for eternity. Your mission, Adam, if you decide to accept it, is to find Eve."

CHAPTER 8

Mother Nature, a mind concept who traveled by force of air, was spiteful and malicious with a heart of stone. She was fiendish with diabolical thoughts of keeping Adam and Eve separated forever. Her mind was superior, proven by her creation of animals, but she was in fact ruthless and ill-natured. Mother Nature had the mentality of a spinster and of course, was celibate. She was produced by the Big Bang effect before GOD and the Devil were created.

She watched Eve "connect" with her animals in an innocent, high spirited way and became quite jealous observing this transformation in her animals. The Devil was a decoy in the tree of Good and Evil and was intent on tricking Eve. She voted for this incident to occur. It was a fatal move for Adam to take a bite of the apple and the moment he attempted to swallow his bite he became baffled and confused. Every time Mother Nature saw a man with an "Adam's apple" she laughed ruthlessly at the thought of Adam. Her cold bloodedness was further proven when Adam and Eve were forced out of the Garden of Eden and left to survive on barren land. Her maliciousness separated Adam and Eve at death and kept them apart for 25 lifetimes on Earth. Their souls returned again and again and again to Earth in an automated fashion. God had finally intervened to allow Fate to bring them together once more.

If Adam were to locate Eve, then she promised God she would go away forever. They would be safe in the divine state of Heaven. She would no longer play a hand in their future. Her purpose in the creation of Nature would be over. She laughed uproariously at her tricks played with human beings. The Hunchback of Notre Dame and John Merrick, the Elephant Man came to mind. They were actually new souls who suffered their first lifetime on Earth as freaks. Her forte was freaks of nature and someday, God willing, she would produce the first hermaphrodite.

CHAPTER 9

Jay Reed was of the opinion his life had reached a cross point, a turning point, to which he could never return to a life of normalcy again. He felt apprehensive and overwhelmed, "understandably so." God had said.

He and God would talk again at nine that night. God had told him earlier there was more to the story of him and Eve. Jay was relieved he wasn't in a battle with Mother Nature. It was a battle, he surmised, against Time. Like searching for a needle in a haystack, but God had promised him clues in regards to finding Eve. A soul mate, he mused. He had never been married and had never had a relationship last longer than 6 months (the length of time he was engaged). Eve, he thought, should be the exact same age as him; 3000 years old. What was she like, he wondered. Again God had promised him a profile of her.

God was also in contact with Eve. He knew her whereabouts, but there were rules. God had given as much information as he could give Jay. Why? Whose rules? He thought, Mother Nature's? He knew he wasn't getting the whole boat of bananas here, the whole story. But tonight he would know. God had told him the main motivating factor was to find Eve and finally reach Heaven. God had told him the average lifetimes a person circled Earth to reach Heaven was eight. He had returned to Earth at least 25 lifetimes! It was his punishment for biting the apple; and it was Mother Nature's idea; vicious bitch he thought.

It was 6:30pm and he was having hunger pains. He decided on grilling a steak with baked potato loaded with butter and sour cream and a garden salad. His mind automatically decided on smoked oysters and red wine to start the meal off, but God had said no more alcohol. He badly needed a drink. His palms were sweating and he felt lightheaded. Withdrawal, he mused. He could still smoke those cancer sticks, which God had said would keep him calm and focused. Jay immediately got up from the family room couch and headed towards the kitchen to fix his dinner.

8:50pm – Jay was alone in the house giving his bodyguards the night off as God had instructed. At precisely nine pm when his grandfather's clock chimed nine times God made his presence known. Jay was having a cigarette.

GOD: "Having second thoughts?"

JAY: "I have questions."

GOD: "Shoot."

JAY: "First off what are my chances of finding Eve?"

GOD: "Slim, next question."

JAY: "Will I be in battle with Mother Nature to find Eve?"

GOD: "No. She simply observes now."

JAY: "What clues can you give me to find her?"

GOD: "They're abstract. I'll give you a profile now:

Eve was raised in a poor family environment. Her mother was an alcoholic, abusive and neglectful towards her. Her father left Eve and her mother when she was 6 years old. He was a pharmaceutical salesman and never established contact with them after he left them. Eve adapted poorly in school and didn't have any friends throughout her elementary and teen-age years. At the age of twenty I came to her and led her to better surroundings, where she still remains. That location is top secret. She has repulsive reoccurring nightmares of snakes. She imagines in her dreams of biting the apple again. Eve has integrity and high morals. She's never been with a man. She is as pure as a full-blooded thoroughbred, sinless, and wholesome."

JAY: "Does she know about me?" Stupid question he thought.

GOD: "Yes. In her dreams she sees a blurry face of a man biting into an apple and then she usually wakes up. She knows you'll be in search of her now."

JAY: "What does she look like?"

GOD: "She's beautiful. Big baby blue eyes, blond hair to her waist, and a Playboy's playmate figure. Now here is an important clue. She's in the animal world. She is surrounded by animals. So, start a list now of occupations where animals are involved."

JAY: "Anything else?

GOD: "That's all for now on Eve."

Jay pondered what he'd just been told then asked

"Whose rules about this situation are you following, Mother Nature's?"

GOD: "I state the rules, Adam."

JAY: "Go on" he said with the impatience of a young child wanting his favorite story to be read.

GOD: "Patience is a virtue."

Jay smiled and said "Is there a time limit in finding her?"

GOD: "You have until death…he replied."

JAY: "Where should I start?" His voice wavered.

GOD: "Start by making a list of the occupations where there are animals."

JAY: "I have an idea!" he exclaimed suddenly snapping his fingers. "What about the zoo?"

GOD: "Ransack your mind with ideas."

JAY: "Now I have all the dozen eggs in a carton? You've told me everything?"

GOD: "No. There is another presence in this plot- the Devil."

Jay paused for a moment taking this new information in, then his jaw dropped.

God was silent.

Jay regained his composure and exclaimed "The Devil!"

GOD: "Bulls-eye, affirmative. There is yet another entanglement."

JAY: "Who?" He asked hurriedly.

GOD: "Didn't your mother teach you patience?"

Jay laughed loudly, paused then said "Who?" again.

GOD: "The Devil can't see you now, but he knows who you are: a movie star."

JAY: "What part does the Devil have in this story?"

GOD: "We've made a bet. I'm counting on you to get to Eve first. You have a competitor, Adam. "

JAY: "Who?" He repeated for the third time.

GOD: "Drake Roberson is on the warpath to find Eve. He's being guided by the Devil. Roberson is the Anti-Christ."

CHAPTER 10

Jay Reed was flabbergasted and began pacing the floor in his living room muttering something about the end of the world. God was silent through this. "What have I gotten myself into" Jay exclaimed.

"Only God knows" was the answer from the Supreme Being.

"Drake Roberson!" he wildly exclaimed. "The billionaire is… is… is the Anti-Christ?"

"Affirmative" was God's only reply. "Now sit down and listen now. He knows all about you. He knows all about you from your beginning. People magazine has been very kind to him, filling in all the aspects of your life starting from the point of getting a baseball and bat lain in your crib to your meanderings with women.

Roberson plans to let Eve know who you are and all your exploits with the opposite sex! She'll be mortified and he's counting on that! Now, sit down."

Jay immediately dropped to the floor and sat Indian style on a large pillow. He was still shaking his head.

"Listen carefully… Drake Roberson was born somewhere in Europe. Generations of his family had planned diligently for his birth by passing a book along to each generation foretelling his arrival. The families had been guided by an "unknown presence" using the same mental telepathy I've been using with you.

The book was written and copied from the pages of the last chapter of the Bible; Revelations."

GOD then quoted "And he laid hold on the dragon, that old serpent, which is the Devil and Satan, and bound him a thousand years. And cast him into the bottomless pit, and shut him up, and set a seal upon him, that he should deceive the nations no more, till the thousand years should be fulfilled and after he must be loosed a little season. And when the thousand years are expired, Satan should be loosed out of his prison."

God stopped here for a second then said, "The Devil was planning a comeback also." Jay felt cold chills run through him. God continued "Roberson was born into an unusual household; all of them were Devil Worshippers. He was identified as a newborn by the numbers 666 embedded on his scalp, the mark of the Devil".

God again quoted Revelations, "Here is wisdom. Let him that hath understanding count the number of the beast; for it is the number of a man and his number is six hundred threescore and six".

God continued, "He was born into a family of aristocrats and it was an unusual household that raised him. Present and living in his house was the physician who delivered him, the nurse who assisted in his birth, his parents, a housekeeper and a nanny.

The nanny, who was an evil woman, taught him to

be extremely aggressive with his playmates and guarded him from being "brain washed" by the teachings of his Sunday school class. However, he was taught religion, only it wasn't about Jesus Christ who was exemplified, but the writings of the Beast in Revelations.

By age 10 he was aware of his importance in regards to the history of the Earth and its final battle and outcome; being total destruction of the planet. He knew he would battle Jesus Christ for dominion over the world.

His nanny selected his friends carefully and playtime was monitored by her. She taught him to steal toys, bargain over them, and take them away from his playmates.

Roberson never went to school until age 13. Before then he was given homebound instruction from a learned professor. At 13 he entered Young's Military Academy to learn discipline.

The academy was run like a boot camp, and had a stringent schedule to follow. Roberson was up at four a.m. and would run five miles, then study at seven until breakfast. At eight he cleaned his room, polished his shoes, and did his laundry. From nine am to three pm classes were held. At four he had dinner, and bedtime was at nine pm.

His curriculum included two foreign languages, French and German both of which he now speaks fluently. In addition to those languages, he also had a tutor who assisted him in learning Chinese and Japanese as well. It has helped him in oversea dealings that he has."

Jay was feeling sick to his stomach by now.

God noticing that, said: "Should I go on?"

He nodded back.

God continued. "At the age of nineteen he then

entered Harvard Business College, where he carried a full load. He studied World History, Politics, Economics, Psychology, and Criminology. The most chilling part comes in here. Are you ready for it?"

Jay nodded, completely flabbergasted at the history of this man. "I can't tell you exactly, but there are still open files at FBI headquarters about what happened to his family. His mother committed suicide by jumping out of their two story house. Foul play, however, was suspected, and Roberson, being home on leave from school was suspected in pushing his mother out the window, but it was never proven.

The nanny had an "accident" by falling down the stairs and breaking her neck. His aunt and uncle disappeared one day, and they were never found again. His father reportedly fatally shot himself with a shotgun while hunting with whom else but Roberson.

CHAPTER 11

Phoebe Miles was a stunner and the mistress of Drake Roberson. She had dark red hair, a flawless complexion, piercing hazel eyes, and was as statuesque as a model. She called herself a clairvoyant and was so successful in what she did that it was her livelihood. Her career was so well known she did psychic readings sometimes for the police and had helped in bringing criminals to justice. Several times she was called to the murder scene to provide the authorities with a "profile" of the killer. Phoebe had an offer by a television network to do readings in an hour slot during prime time. She was considering the offer.

She met Drake Roberson at a party hosted by a famous film director and it was love at first sight three years ago for them. They'd been together ever since. Phoebe often helped Drake Roberson in his business dealings by figuring out the weaknesses in his colleagues. She became an asset to Roberson and traveled frequently with him. Sexually she was dynamic. Most times she astounded Roberson with her sexual appetite which was insatiable.

Roberson was sitting behind his desk at New York headquarters reading the Times. Phoebe entered his office and sat down in a chair opposite him. Peering down through his reading glasses he asked "What have you been up to?" "I cancelled my afternoon appointments and went to the horse track.""Lost $500.00" she replied.

Roberson got up and went to the bar and poured himself a martini. "Drown your sorrows?" he asked her, holding up a wine glass.

"Chablis" she simply said. For the next hour Phoebe and Roberson discussed his latest business venture. He was considering opening a clinic to test for AIDS with the johns who frequented his prostitutes. "Well, the girls will breathe a sigh of relief" Phoebe said approvingly. She waited for his reply and glanced at him to find him staring at the floor, lost in thought.

"What's on your mind, Drake?" As she asked this her eyes squinted slightly. Roberson was thinking about the race between him and Jay Reed. Phoebe was perceptive enough to know Roberson had something on his mind, but she would never guess exactly what.

She might have surmised it had to do with another woman, but that was all.

Roberson was always seen in public with beautiful women as an escort, but Phoebe felt secure; he was faithful to her. They had kept their affair private for the last 3 years because it might have affected her career. Even though Roberson still found Phoebe Miles exciting, he frequently played with an idea in his mind of a fresh, young, beautiful body beneath him... Eve.

Once he found Eve he would build an empire with her. Phoebe was considered dispensable now. She didn't know he was the Anti-Christ. That was top secret between him and the Devil.

Roberson had plans to become an even bigger icon than he already was. He got up from his chair and Phoebe arose to face him. He kissed her ardently and then ripped off her blouse, unzipped her jeans, and pulled them down. Phoebe gave a sharp intake of breath at his sudden movements. He forced her to the floor, spread her legs, and began to thrust fast and hard inside of her.

She winced and cried out in pain because of his roughness. He came quickly in an explosion of pleasure and then rolled over laughing beside her. "Drake, what has gotten into you?" she asked breathless. Roberson laughed inwardly and knew soon he would be rid of Ms. Phoebe Miles.

CHAPTER 12

Sitting on a void planet far below the Heavens and Earth sat a Demon. He was precariously observing Drake Roberson in his study smoking a cigarette and reading the New York Times on Earth, which was the Devil's playground. He was brutal, savage, and diabolical.

In medieval times he had seen his work; people driven mad with mental illnesses and placed in asylums. They were chained to their beds, starved, and beaten. He had cast spells on young women in those times and the Catholic Church had resorted to exorcisms to relieve them of possession.

Now his time had come. Roberson was his king on the chessboard and Eve his queen. The Devil had made a deal with Roberson. It was a contract written with a thumbprint of Drake Roberson's own blood meaning that if he captured Eve and procreated a son, the Devil's promise to him was to make Roberson a "maverick" in the world of politics from governor to senator to the Presidency of the United States.

Roberson had sold his soul to the Devil for this. If

Drake didn't reach Eve before Adam, his soul would be lost in Purgatory for about a year. He thought of Roberson as gullible and greedy. His own greed was blinding him to the fact that God himself was guiding Adam.

He chuckled maliciously. Then his face was stone again. It was a poker face. He was bitter with a black heart. The Devil had waited patiently for his prey since the fall of mankind in the Garden of Eden. He spitefully mused over the fact that more people were coming into their own with the teachings of Jesus Christ and ascending to Heaven on the average of 6 to 7 times around the face of the Earth. God's plan was to return Jesus Christ to Earth and begin the Second Coming in approximately one hundred years.

The Devil whined, then produced an evil laugh that sometimes sent chills down Roberson's back. He wanted to create mayhem on Earth of harm, violence, and destruction.

The Devil had witnessed mankind's violence. He had been there when Hitler had sent millions of humans to the gas chamber. He had seen the Jews in concentration camps starved to death; their bodies piled high in wagons as mere skeletons. The Vietnam War evoked pure hatred in humans. POWs were violently sentenced to mental and physical abuse living in huts, whipped, starved, forsaken. He had no respect for mankind. The downfall of man began in Eden where his work had started.

If Roberson failed him, he would have to, on a "gentleman's agreement", slither away, defeated. From Revelations he recalled..."And the devil that deceived them was cast into the lake of fire and brimstone, where the beast and the false prophet are and shall be tormented day and night forever and ever."

"Amen" he said bitterly.

CHAPTER 13

One a.m.: God had left at midnight and Adam was in a stupor. He hadn't been able to get past the fact that Drake Roberson was the Anti-Christ and competing for Eve! His Eve, he thought, "I'm Adam" he said in wonderment, then laughed hysterically. He got up from the couch and was stupefied again. He sat down quickly, missed the couch, and ended up on the floor. He needed a drink. "Nope", he said out loud. He had promised God: no liquor. He looked towards the bar then heard a low chuckle.

"Have one for the road ahead" God's voice boomed.

Adam jumped up and poured himself a shot of whiskey downing it in one gulp. He felt better trying to reassure himself. "First things first, and last of all, the first thing I need is another drink last of all" he said out loud. He laughed at his own joke. Now where in this world is Eve he thought to himself.

He fell over laughing again. Then he rolled his eyes to the ceiling. This can't be happening he thought. Then he shook his head at the magnitude of it all again. First God, then Eve, then Mother Nature, now Roberson and the Devil! He picked up a cigarette and missed lighting it twice. Inwardly he was confused and scared. Roberson knows who I am. Why not a showdown now, he pondered? Why doesn't one of his thugs show up and send me to a quiet place in a cemetery, or put me at the bottom of the river, or send me a one-way plane ticket to Greenland he thought. But he followed the rules. It was a battle of wits. Instead of facing each other, they were running parallel in a marathon race to find Eve.

Adam went to his den and sat at his desk. He turned the banker's lamp on and took pen and paper in hand and wrote the following:

ADAM'S LIST TO FIND EVE

1. Ringling Brothers Circus
2. Animal psychics on TV
3. The horse track
4. The zoo
5. Animal trainers in Hollywood
6. Humane Society of the United States
7. People for the Ethical Treatment of Animals
8. Cable's Animal Planet

God had told him Eve was with animals in a huge way. Adam had no clue how close Roberson was to finding her, but God had warned him of "tricks" he might pull. "Anything goes" God had told him. Looking over his list, he was pleased.

"Off to a great start" he thought satisfied with himself.

CHAPTER 14

Adam thought he had some tricks up his sleeve and laughed inwardly. He headed south in his Mercedes and in 30 minutes he was at the largest pet store in Hollywood, Klein's Pet Place. He walked in and went over to the reptile exhibit.

There were iguanas, several different species of lizards, and a snake exhibit. Before him in a glass cage, coiled on a large branch was a 6-foot boa constrictor. "Female boa, very tame, $300 the sign on the glass read. A girl with brunette hair in a ponytail and a pierced lip came over to him and asked if he needed any help.

Adam pointed to the boa and said he wanted to handle her. The girl lifted the glass top and retrieved the boa. She placed the 20 pound snake in his hands. Adam had never handled a snake before and it sent chills through him when the boa began moving and wrapping the bottom half of its body around his waist. The girl began petting the snake's head and said in an endearing way "She is quite tame".

"How do you feed her and what do you feed her?" Adam asked.

He was repulsed at the idea of offering the reptile something live for dinner.

"She is on a diet of frozen mice" the girl informed him. "You can thaw the mice, place her and the mice in a large trash bag and gently shake the bag. She'll consume them."

"Perfect." Adam thought relieved. He purchased the $300 snake with a month's supply of frozen mice for dinners.

Adam went home with his new pet and got on the Internet in his den. The Ringling Brothers Circus tour came up on his computer screen. They were playing in Chicago, his hometown, all that week. He hurriedly packed his bags, and gathered the large reptile in a suitcase.

He got in his car and headed to the airport. He had called the airport from his condo and when he pulled into the parking lot he observed that his jet was already on the runway with a crew of three men standing by. He boarded his jet and sat in the pilot's seat. The crew had already checked the engine and put a full tank of fuel in it.

He taxied the jet down the runway and eventually got flight clearance.

Five hours later he landed his jet at the airport in Chicago. At 3 pm he checked into a hotel and ordered room service. Three hours later he was at the Ringling Brothers Circus with suitcase in hand.

Claiming to be the largest circus in the world, Adam was overwhelmed with the sights and sounds of the event.

He sat through the bear act, dog tricks, and the elephant parade.

The finale was a wild cat act and he noticed a pretty blond outside the huge cage carrying a whip. She walked into the cage and Adam retrieved a pair of binoculars from around his neck and checked her out.

Up close he surmised the girl was in her 20s with a long blond braid. She was wearing a brief blue sequined outfit. The pretty girl walked inside the cage and snapped her whip at the four wild cats. During the course of her act she commanded them to walk in a circle around her, climb stairs, and jump through burning hoops.

The circus event ended with a huge animal parade with clowns. At the close of the act Adam decided to make his move. He reached for the suitcase and saw that the locks had been busted open. The snake was missing!

Suddenly two rows in front of him he heard screams and noticed people moving quickly away from their seats. At that moment he knew the location of the 6-foot boa.

He jumped two rows in front of him and spotted the snake. It was slowly moving towards the row below. Jay was within arms length of the snake now and reached out and grasped its tail, using his other hand to get a good grip on her.

Greatly relieved at finding her, he sat down on the bleacher seat and held onto her for dear life.

People had started to evacuate the huge circus tent and in front of the stage he noticed several security guards. Gathering his wits he got up and headed back stage.

A guard stopped him. This is where fame comes in handy he thought. "I'm Jay Reed," he said to the security guard "and I need to get back stage." The guard looked him up and down and at the snake for a moment, and then said "Go on back."

Backstage, Adam was surrounded by a multitude of tents and trailers. He passed by a clown with a painted face in a red jumpsuit and enormous feet and stopped him. "I'm looking for a girl," he began. "Aren't we all, buddy?" the clown retorted.

Noticing the snake the clown asked "Are you a new act?" "No" Adam said. "I'm with the zoo. Now which tent occupies the girl in the big cat act?" The clown motioned with his hand to a large blue trailer at the end of the line of RV's. "Thanks" Adam said. "No problem" the clown answered spitting a spew of tobacco to the ground.

Adam paced himself now. What was next, he mused. He knocked on the trailer's door and heard a female voice say "C'mon in." He opened the door and stood there with the boa draped around his neck. "Who the hell are you?" the pretty girl asked in an accusing tone. "I'm Adam, are you Eve?" "W-what!" the girl said rising and reaching over to slap his face.

CHAPTER 15

Drake Roberson's headquarters was in Chicago. It was a two-story building overlooking a 3-acre lake and 20 acres of hills and woods. The first floor contained 5 large offices and within the center was an enormous conference room with skylights. Roberson dominated the second floor.

His office contained a large cherry wood desk, marble fireplace, two black leather couches and two leather recliners. On one side of the massive room were a 55 gallon salt water aquarium and a bookshelf.

He had collected such books as The Abnormal Brain, The Business Man's Almanac, Donald Trump's Autobiography, 101 Ways to Get the Deal of the Century, Business Deals and Marketing Strategies, and the Holy Bible.

Behind Roberson's desk were two marble statues of Greek Gods. In the center of the office was a chessboard on a table with two cherry wood chairs on either side. There was a globe lamp overhead. A doorway behind his desk led to a full size kitchen with an island, bathroom equipped with a Jacuzzi, and a bedroom with a king size waterbed.

When working late at night, he often bedded there and brought Phoebe Miles there for long weekends. His wife had joined AA, but the nagging and bitching hadn't stopped so he entertained the thought of moving into his headquarters permanently.

Tonight he was sitting at his desk looking over his account's bookkeeping records concerning Roberson's Sleep Inn in New York. He barely studied what he was reading.

He was waiting for a visit from the Devil. Roberson knew he could observe him at any time and read his thoughts. He was a private person and at first found this disconcerting. He was careful about what thoughts he did have.

Thirty minutes later the lights suddenly went out except for the overhead light over the chess table. He blinked twice attempting to adjust his eyes to the darkness. "Pssst…Roberson" the Devil hissed.

Roberson "Present" he said.

Devil: "Reed has a list the length of his arm." he said in a hoarse whisper.

Roberson: "I'm looking into humane societies in major cities; New York, Chicago, Los…"

Devil: "Hey, diddle, diddle, the cat and the fiddle…"

Roberson: continued…" Angeles"

Devil: "The cow jumped over the moon? Did you ever graduate from kindergarten, Roberson?"

Roberson remained silent.

Devil: "Fool-you're in the big leagues now, get neck and neck with him at least!"

Roberson: "Where has he been?"

Devil: "I hate fair fights… the rules you know, I can't tell you. The little dog laughed to see such a sport."

Roberson: "And the dish ran away with the spoon" he finished.

The Devil lit up a cigarette. He called it his "social habit".

Roberson: "I can out think him."

Devil: "Lizzy Borden took an axe and gave her mother 40 whacks. Your nanny's back was broken in 3 places aside from her neck."

Roberson squirmed in his chair.

Devil: "Step on a crack, break your mother's back."

Roberson remained silent.

Devil: "Tail him; find out where he goes and who he talks to."

Roberson: "But there are rules to follow in this."

Devil: "I cheat and God knows it. Try to be inconspicuous. Those thugs of yours stand out in any crowd."

Roberson: "I have a new man I can put on it."

The Devil pulled out a coin from behind his ear then sent the coin into a spin. "Head's I win, tails you lose." He chuckled maliciously. "I expect a full report on Reed in 48 hours."

Roberson shuddered.

Devil: "Out think him Roberson! He's just doing child's play now."

The Devil was gone.

He had 48 hours to find out what Reed was up to.

CHAPTER 16

After the incident at the Ringling Brothers Circus, Adam decided to sit tight at home and use his wits by bringing Eve to him.

Through the internet he ordered a tape of all the animal psychics on cable, the Animal Planet episodes, and a taped Jay Leno Tonight Show of the girl at the San Diego Zoo, plus a documentary of all the animal trainers in Hollywood.

He also had a tape on speeches made by the Humane Society of the United State's most prominent speakers and a tape made by the People for Ethical Treatment of Animals reporting on animal abuse and neglect.

Through the course of the day and night he watched one reel after another. There were a multitude of pretty girls he viewed, but he slowly came to the realization that none of them were Eve.

The girl at the San Diego Zoo actually handled a small king snake. The people viewed on the Humane Society of the United States tape didn't have actual contact with animals; they were merely figureheads for the organization. Cruelty investigations performed by the People for Ethical Treatment of Animals were done by males.

He concluded he had reached a dead end.

At that exact moment God appeared.

GOD: "You've done well in narrowing the leads."

ADAM: "Damn it."

GOD: "A word of warning here… Roberson is playing dirty pool."

ADAM: "Meaning what?"

GOD: "Roberson and the Devil have tricks up their sleeves. Use your wits to outsmart them, and be careful."

ADAM: "What?"

GOD: "Espionage", he said, "It is imperative that you find Eve soon. She is in great danger. Her life is at stake. She's being followed by men that are barbaric, brutal, and savage. Roberson has been told the same message… there's a clue. Use your wits!"

ADAM: "I've exhausted my list with the exception of the horse track."

GOD: "Cancel the horse track. Eve isn't anywhere animals are being exploited. Let Roberson waste his time there."

Adam paused a moment- something sounded so familiar to him with the clue God had just given him. It was on the tip of his tongue, but he couldn't place the memory."

GOD: "He is a very devious man. Again be careful, Adam."

And with that God was gone.

Eve was in danger with evil men. Adam mused throughout the night and ruminated over what God had said. He had a feeling there was a situation someone else had been in similar to Eve, but nothing came to mind. He eventually went to sleep on the couch.

Meanwhile Rick Sampson, one of Roberson's men, sat in a car outside his house. "He hasn't gone anywhere today or tonight" he said into his cell phone.

Adam woke up several times during the course of the night. He had a nagging thought in relation to Eve and her situation. He finally gave up trying to retrieve the thought and slept through the morning till noon.

At one pm Adam's two bodyguards walked into the living room. Adam told them to take the day off. Unaware he was being watched by Drake's employee; Adam got up and went to the kitchen to make some coffee.

While preparing the coffee, Adam knew in a flash the whereabouts of Eve. He had dreamed of gorillas and a blur of a face. The face was clear to him… Sigourney Weaver the Hollywood actress in "Gorillas in the Mist".

It was a true story of a woman who was trying to save a family of gorillas and was harassed by poachers who eventually murdered her.

Eve must be in Africa he thought. He waited for God to make his presence known.

CHAPTER 17

At the precise moment when Adam came to the realization Eve might be in Africa, God was with her. Eve was having a nightmare. She tossed and turned in her bed and envisioned a snake coiled on a branch of a tree saying "Eat the apple, Eve, you can live forever. In her dream she plucked the apple from the tree and bit into it. Then she thought she heard the footsteps of God entering the Garden of Eden.

GOD: "Eve…"he said softly. "Wake up."

Eve's eyelids fluttered and eventually she opened her eyes.

EVE: "They're close and getting closer" she said.

GOD: "Adam knows your whereabouts. It's just a matter of time now. Don't venture out too far from the village."

EVE: "Dawn is near giving birth to her baby. I must check on her every day, she's so close."

God knew who she was referring to. Eve had been

with the female giraffe since the beginning of her gestation period. She was deep in the jungle and Eve knew the jungle like the back of her hand.

GOD: "Be careful. Roberson is tailing Adam. He could be very close. If he finds you, he'll kidnap you! You know that"

EVE: "Yes!"

GOD: "Adam at this point is unaware he's being followed by one of Roberson's men. He could lead them right to you".

EVE: "I'll be careful, watchful."

GOD: "I'll leave you now.

God left her and returned to Adam."

Adam had already phoned the airport's small plane division and alerted them to get his jet ready for takeoff. He packed his bag and pulled from his night stand a small pistol and a magazine of ammunition.

GOD: (As he entered the room), "Beautiful bull's-eye!"

Adam grinned widely and put the pistol and ammunition in his bag.

GOD: "Since you've gotten this far I can tell you she's in Nairobi, Kenya. Now what's your next step?"

Adam paused for a moment then said "I'm going on a tour of Nairobi through a guide that will take me into the bowels of the jungle. I'll find her."

GOD: "What's Drake doing now? THINK! The two

of you will be running parallel to find Eve. How close do you think he is?"

ADAM: "I haven't got a clue. He knows where I live!"

GOD: "Affirmative. So what's he doing now?"

ADAM: "Following me!"

GOD: "Bingo."

ADAM: "But the rules!"

GOD: "The Devil cheats."

ADAM: "I'll sneak out the back door then."

GOD: "Think like Roberson again. What's his next move?"

Adam looked confused. God knew, but Adam didn't know that during the course of the night, Little Bit had broken the house alarm and planted wiring devices in each of his rooms. Rick Sampson took off his ear phones and used his cell phone. "Reed thinks she's in Africa", he said into the phone. "Follow him" Roberson replied. "Don't let him out of your sight!"

Roberson sat back in his chair at his headquarters in Chicago and looked at Dr. Fingers who was sitting across from his desk. "Get a plane ready for Africa", he ordered. Dr. Fingers immediately got up from his chair and left the room.

CHAPTER 18

Drake Roberson was at his headquarters in Chicago waiting for his housekeeper to pack his suitcase. Phoebe Miles walked into his office unexpectedly.

His housekeeper entered the doorway and asked him if he wanted to take his gray suit along. "Where are you going Drake?" Phoebe asked.

"To Africa", he answered and waved his hand up as if to make her go away.

"Is this a new business venture?" Phoebe said.

"Yes, yes I'm buying a new hotel there", he replied. "Do you want me to go along?"

Drake looked up at her and shook his head. Phoebe Miles took a long look at him, her eyes squinted. "You're as nervous as a cat on a hot tin roof, Drake. What gives?" Roberson stood up and pointed his finger at her. "Get out, get out, it's all over!" he exclaimed.

"What's all over?"

"Us, us, we're all over."

"Why, who is she? Have you met someone new?"

Drake took a step for her and shouted "Yes, yes, someone new. Now get out!"

"Who is she?" Phoebe asked stepping forward.

"She's Eve!" Roberson replied.

"Eve who?" Phoebe asked, her voice rising.

"Eve, you know, the Garden of Eden".

Phoebe Miller laughed out loud and said "C'mon Drake, you can do better than that!"

"I can't do better than that! You can't do better than that is what I mean to say: You're out!" he replied pointing to the door again. "Exit bitch!" he added his voice rising to a shrill pitch.

Phoebe Miles stood in wonderment at what was being said. She then picked up a small marble statue on his desk and threw it at him missing his head by an inch. Roberson ducked. "I'm over, huh? Mark my words, Drake Roberson; it's not over until I say it's over. Now who is she?"

"Ever heard of Adam and Eve?" he asked her.

Phoebe Miles looked down at the floor and shook her head in confusion.

"Well, Eve still exists and I'm catching a plane to Africa to find her before Jay Reed does."

"Jay Reed, the actor? What does he have to do with this?" she asked looking more confused.

"You're out of your league, Phoebe. You're small town in this." Roberson said in an exasperated fashion.

Phoebe Miles began to cry and replied "Make sense, Drake. What have you got yourself into?" she said almost begging him to explain.

"He'll make me President one day!" Roberson said matter-of-factly.

"You're planning to become President?" Phoebe looked at him incredulously.

"No, no! Not in this lifetime…The next!"

"What's happening here?" Phoebe's face turned a shade of white and she leaned on his desk for support.

"I'm in the league with the Devil" Roberson said pounding his fist on his desk. When his words finally registered, Phoebe Miles fainted.

CHAPTER 19

GOD: "Mother?"

Mother Nature's visualization comes in. She is a 40ish looking woman with coal black hair tied up in a bun and wearing a Chinese dress.

MOTHER NATURE: "Yes."

GOD: "Adam knows the location of Eve is in Africa."

MOTHER NATURE: "Good God!"

GOD: "I don't really like my name used as a euphemism, Mother. Roberson is in hot pursuit."

MOTHER NATURE: as she laughed wickedly. "That'll take the wind out of his sails." (Meaning Adam)

GOD: "Penny for your thoughts Mother."

MOTHER NATURE: "There is no rest for the wicked (meaning Roberson). He'll pay through the nose if he loses. I'll whistle in the dark."

GOD: "Meaning what?"

MOTHER NATURE: "I'm cheerful in a situation that doesn't warrant optimism God."

GOD: "Eve will be a sight for sore eyes for Adam."

MOTHER NATURE: "Prick"!

GOD: "Watch your tongue Mother."

MOTHER NATURE: "The Devil is at his wits end. Adam had a stroke of luck in finding Eve."

GOD: "I predict he'll have Roberson running like a dog with his tail between his legs."

MOTHER NATURE: "Roberson has rocks in his head. He doesn't see the handwriting on the wall."

GOD: "Will you be there for the final battle?"

MOTHER NATURE: "Wild horses couldn't keep me away", she snorted. "I'm green with envy."

GOD: "You're a wicked, spiteful bitch."

MOTHER NATURE: "In a pig's eye… I'm taking 40 winks now while the show must go on."

GOD: "Roger, Out."

CHAPTER 20

Drew Morris and his crew of five men had been searching for what the natives in the jungle called "the white woman". They had discovered five native tribes and looked in every hut and tent to locate her.

She sabotaged three of their latest ventures in capturing animals for their underground trade. She somehow knew where they were going next and was two days ahead of them.

They had attempted to round up a herd of elephants in order to kill them and extract their ivory tusks, but when they had gotten to their location they were gone. The "white woman" had managed to take them deeper into the jungle and hidden them. The net traps they had laid out for wild cats, leopards, and black panthers, were lying on the ground in shreds.

Drew Morris was furious. It was costing him $1500 a day to keep his men in paychecks. They should have already been through with the captures and at the black market. Looking back he recalled the years he had shot and killed elephants for their tusks. The newspapers had referred to the two hundred dead animals as the "elephant's graveyard" and one man had commented it was the worst case he had seen so far of animal mutilation. The black market paid an enormous price for animal skins of leopards and kept him living a life of luxury.

Morris had been in the poaching business for twenty years and never had trouble like this before. The native police authorities there had once been on his trail and he had backtracked in a circle and was in hot pursuit of the policeman. Morris's men had caught him and methodically proceeded to cut off his ears. He then had one of his men mail the ears to the local police station.

They left the man bleeding and tied to a tree for the animals of the jungle to find. He had killed crocodiles by leaving fish bait in the river then shot them in the head while they feasted on the bait. He had captured monkeys and had them shipped to a research lab in the United States. He snorted loudly when he recalled what kind of experiments they performed on them.

The Humane Society of the United States eventually discovered the lab and found blood on the chairs where the monkeys had been tied down. The monkeys were given shock treatments, but they were rescued during a raid on the place.

He took special delight skinning wild cats. Just for fun he had shot and killed a lioness and her 2 cubs.

When he found the "white woman" he planned to first cut off her arms and legs and finally bludgeon her eyes out. Morris would stop at nothing to find her. He knew they were getting closer.

CHAPTER 21

Adam landed at the airport in Nairobi 24 hours later after a stop in Amsterdam and checked into a hotel. He took a quick shower and then returned to the main lobby and stood at the front desk. The clerk looked like an African native, and wore a wooden lion on a chain around his neck.

"I want to know who gives tours here," Adam said. The clerk looked him over and then pulled out several brochures from a desk drawer and handed them to him. "Thanks", he said and headed back to his hotel room. It seemed likely that Eve was working as a tour guide here in Kenya or close by. He scanned the brochures. There were five of them.

He returned to the lobby and asked about the tour guides. He described Eve to the desk clerk and the man slowly shook his head. "No. No one I know looks like that. Adam was deeply disappointed and thought to himself, "back to the drawing board."

He went back to his hotel room and lay down. What

other occupations could there be? He thought maybe she was employed at the local zoo, but he discarded the idea since God had told him that she wasn't involved with any exploitation of animals.

Drake Roberson was standing in the front hotel lobby of the Royal Hotel signing the register. His suitcases were carried by Dr. Fingers and he promptly picked them up and followed Roberson to room 409. He passed by Adam's room.

Adam decided to get some dinner and wondered when God would show up again. He was running out of leads . The Royal Hotel had a large restaurant advertising the native food.

He entered the restaurant and thought maybe he should ask around town with a description of Eve, but then decided he would start his investigation tomorrow. It was a massive room with tables and booths lighted by candles.

He was ushered in by a tall, lean hostess attired in a blue and white uniform and white apron. There was a live band there playing African music to the beat of drums. He requested a booth by the band and was ushered to one close to them. He was handed a menu by the hostess and was attempting to make a decision when he looked up and saw Drake Roberson and a tall, grotesque looking man entering the restaurant.

Roberson scanned the room briefly and then he looked straight at Adam. Their eyes locked for a moment. Roberson had a dead pan look.

Adam's eyes never wavered from him. Then the hostess came forward and led Roberson and his bodyguard to a table near Adam's booth.

Adam felt a chill of excitement at seeing him. "He may not yet have a clue to where Eve is and is tailing me", he thought. He decided he would disappear before Roberson finished his meal.

He is at the same hotel, he thought, better change hotels.

He ordered his meal and then sat there watching Roberson out of the corner of his eye.

Roberson's eyes never met his again. "Arrogant bastard", Adam thought and waited for his meal which was the special of the day.

CHAPTER 22

Two men were seated by the hostess in the next booth. Adam could vaguely hear their conversation as one them said, "I've never seen anything like it, she actually had the boar hypnotized."

"Really," the second man replied.

Adam could tell both of the men were drunk by the way they slurred their speech.

"Then she gave hand signals to some chimps that were hanging out in the trees and they started yakking away."

"How much did it cost you," the second man asked. The first man, ignoring the question, said "Then she wrestled with one of the female lions, while the male watched her from about one hundred feet". Adam felt a growing excitement and then continued eavesdropping. "It was major bucks, but worth it".

Adam could not stand it a minute longer. He got up, and approached the two men. "I couldn't help overhearing your conversation, but whom are you talking about?" he asked them.

The first man stuttered "I'm not allowed to give out that kind of information. It's a private tour... only for the upper crust. Get lost buddy".

Adam tried again to get information out of the first man, but he refused to speak further to him.

Roberson was then watching Adam closely with a curious expression on his face. Adam smirked at him, paid his bill, and left the restaurant.

In his hotel room GOD appeared.

God: "You're getting warmer, Adam. That was a twist of fate you overheard those two men."

Adam:" She gives tours."

God: "All the money goes to preserving land for her animals and stopping poachers. She gives large amounts of money to the government to assist authorities in finding men who kill hundreds, thousands, of elephants and big cats each year. You're close now, but be careful. Roberson is just down the hall from you. Lose him somehow."

The next day Adam arose around 5am, ordered toast and coffee from room service, then took a hot shower. He left the hotel via the fire exit to lose Roberson's bodyguard and went to the local bank. He transferred one million dollars from his bank in Hollywood to the bank in Nairobi.

The president of the bank was kind enough to loan him a briefcase so he could travel inconspicuously with the money. Adam went to the main street in Nairobi and began canvassing with the money. He stopped in several hotels, two restaurants, and two grocery stores.

Each time he asked for the name of the woman who gave private tours, then would open the briefcase to show he meant business in finding her and had the cash to pay for her tour. Everyone was tight lipped about it. No one would tell him. Finally disgusted and disillusioned he went back to the hotel.

A different desk clerk observing him, gave him a wide smile, and asked what his business was in Kenya.

"Aren't you Jay Reed?" he asked Adam.

He nodded.

"Well, welcome to Kenya. Is this your first trip here?"

Adam said "Yes".

"You look like you've just lost your best friend. What's the matter?" the clerk asked.

Adam, dejected, told him he was looking for a woman who gave exclusive tours in Kenya.

"Well, that would be Nature's Way".

Adam blinked then said "What?"

"Yes," the man replied "It's a top secret operation, only for the elite".

"Do you know the woman?" Adam asked the clerk.

"Yes, she's quite popular here".

"I didn't have any luck with the people here," Adam said.

"Word is out around here she's in trouble with Morris and everyone is trying to protect her by keeping their mouths shut."

"Whose is Morris?" Adam asked.

"He's the meanest, baddest man around these parts, a famous poacher."

Adam felt cold chills down his spine. "How can I find her?"

"She lives in a village with a tribe south of here, some 150 miles away. I don't know which tribe exactly. She keeps well hidden."

"South of here?" Adam repeated and waited for the man to acknowledge it. The man merely nodded.

Adam decided not to check out of the hotel in case Roberson was trailing him. He glanced around to see if anyone was following him. Seeing no one he placed a call in the hotel lobby to Kenya's airport and instructed the employee to have a crew alerted and on standby for him to pick up his jet. He then had the desk clerk call him a taxi and in 30 minutes he was on his way to the airport.

At the airport he asked the girl behind the desk what tribes could be found south approximately 150 miles away? She looked bored and stated that there were several, but didn't know they're exact location.

Boarding the jet, Adam waved a show of thanks to the crew and taxied down the runway.

CHAPTER 23

He had gone approximately 100 miles and could see nothing but acres of land and some wooded areas. Disappointed he decided to head farther south to see what he could find there. I'm merely sightseeing he thought disgusted again. He decided to plug in a cd.

A song by Savage Garden came on as he glided in the air. He sang along with the song as he thought of Eve.

Adam turned the CD on louder, then sat up straight in his seat like a rocket. Over a tract of land he spotted a jeep with a blond in it and another jeep in hot pursuit after her about 500 feet away. Both vehicles were traveling at a fast rate of speed and the second jeep was gaining on her.

Adam pulled out his gun from the storage compartment, unholstered it , pushed the safety off, and cocked the gun.

Slowing down and guiding the jet lower to the ground, he could see the second jeep had five men and one driver. They had guns and were firing at the jeep ahead.

Using his Heads-Up Display he fired a spray of bullets

into the rear tires of the second jeep and it swerved and then flipped over. The men in the jeep managed to get out and were still shooting at the girl. Adam lowered the jet to ground level and slowed his rate of speed.

The girl in the jeep, witnessing her rescue, waved, got out of her vehicle and climbed onto the left wing of the jet. The men were now running towards her and firing their guns. Adam made a u-turn with the jet and headed north. He kept the jet at slow speed hoping the girl could hang on.

Gradually she managed to get inside of the jet and Adam took off full speed ahead, leaving the men behind cursing and swearing. The beautiful girl used hand signals over the roar of the jet to guide him where she wanted him to go and eventually, about 50 miles away she signaled him to land near a small forest of trees and what looked like a small village.

CHAPTER 24

Adam safely landed the jet and climbed out only to face the barrel of a shotgun aimed at his nose by One Eye Jack. The blonde got out of the jet and her eyes widened when she spotted Drake Roberson standing two feet behind his sidekick.

"Welcome home, Eve" Roberson bellowed and continued "We've all been waiting for you."

"How did you find her?" Adam asked him despairingly.

"Easy," Roberson said, "The two men at the restaurant were given the third degree by yours truly.

Held at knifepoint, they were easy prey after one of his fingers was cut off,then we showed them Dr. Finger's left hand." Roberson chuckled maliciously then went on… "We found out about the tour of Nature's Way, and paid a cool million to find out from Kenya's greediest native where she lives, and viola, the rest is history."

Roberson gave Adam a devilish grin. One Eye Jack tied Adam's hands behind his back with twine and then tied him to a tree. Adam watched as One Eye Jack assisted Eve into the small two-engine plane with Roberson following her.

He watched them take off heading north to Nairobi. There were natives there standing in a group watching Adam suspiciously. Eventually they left him and began to make a campfire.

Before long he found his voice and said "Does anyone speak English?"

"Nope" one young male said and then laughed.

They all ignored him and gathered around the campfire. Adam was left alone.

As Roberson and his sidekicks, One Eye Jack and Dr. Fingers, took Eve towards Nairobi's airport to transfer to Roberson's private 747, Adam became panic stricken. He was in total darkness and the campfire was burning embers. The natives had left and retired to their huts.

He had reached Eve first, but was it fair play to have kidnapped her? God had warned him several times about Drake Roberson's ingenuity.

"Out think him", God had said.

Why hadn't he been prepared for this? His gun was lying on the seat of the airplane. It was no use to him now. He noticed the moon was full and there were a million stars in the sky. Adam could hear in the distance a pack of hyenas howling mournfully.

In the huts he could see small illuminated lights in each one of them. Why didn't the natives rescue him? He surmised they may be thinking he had tried to kidnap Eve or was a member of Drew Morris's crew. Either way he was tied to the tree. He attempted to wriggle his wrists, but the twine was so tight he couldn't break loose. His hands were numb.

God arrived shortly after midnight.

Adam: "Where have you been?" he said in a weak voice.."They've got Eve".

God: "Silence, calm yourself."

Just then God relaxed Adam and he felt every muscle in his body go limp.

God: "You're in a hell of a predicament." he chuckled softly.

Adam: "What am I supposed to do now?" he said disdainfully.

God: "Listen carefully, I've been in conference with the Devil, we're calling it a tie. You reached Eve first, but Roberson outsmarted you. She's safe. Robinson had to relinquish her at the Royal and she's in a hotel room there. Roberson was ordered to stay at the hotel also, but in a different room."

Adam: "What happens next?"

God: "I'll give you further instructions once you reach the Royal. The both of you have been given a reprieve and have 24 hours to prepare for battle."

Adam wriggled his wrists again.

God laughed uproariously. "I'll perform one of my many miracles. I'll use telekinesis to release you. Stand by."

A moment passed and then Adam felt the twine start to unravel until it was completely untied. He felt a great sense of relief, took the twine off his wrists, and rubbed them dubiously.

God: "Now get your sorry ass in that jet and get to the Royal." he boomed.

CHAPTER 25

The next day at 6am Adam was awakened by God.

God: "You have the next 24 hours to rest before the battle with Roberson."

Adam rubbed the sleep from his eyes, blinked twice, then sat straight up in his bed.

Adam: "What?"

God: "The Devil is preparing Roberson now. Listen carefully, he continued. What you and Roberson will engage in is a battle of wits. It's like a video game; it's called psychic war. There are no rules. No restraints. The motto is "anything goes". I'll open up a pathway to both of your minds. You'll be within 5 feet of each other.

Adam: "You mean we'll fight? But how?" he asked with frown upon his face.

God: "You'll be in a battle with him within your mind. Axes, knives, guns, anything can be used. You won't feel anything. It is all mental power which you will use. You can't touch him. There is no physical contact to be made. If it comes to a tie again, myself and the Devil will decide the winner by the number of hits made. Do you understand?"

Adam: "I think so."

God: "One more thing. The both of you are able to send a message to Eve before the battle begins. I can tell you Roberson sent her a song in the form of a poem. He's attempting to seduce her. So think of a poem, any poem, and I'll pass it through to her."

Adam: "Alright." he agreed.

God: "The important thing now is to rest your mind and prepare for war! I'll be back before the 24 hours is up."

With that God left the room.

Drake had already written his poem :

I don't believe in Paradise
I don't believe in fate
I don't believe in love
As a supernatural state

Love is a chemical reaction
Love is a mutual attraction
Love is infatuation
Love is adoration

I'll love you madly for a lifetime
Then we go our separate ways
I'll end for now
And wait for you
That's all I have to say

He was ready for war. He had eaten breakfast and had done 100 pushups that morning. His mind was clear.

God had talked to Eve. She was sitting in a chair in her hotel room and drinking black coffee when God arrived.

God: "Eve, sweetheart, how are you?"

Eve: "I must get to Dawn; she's ready to deliver any minute now."

God: "I just checked on her. She's not ready yet. You can't leave the hotel. Morris is looking for you now. He's on a warpath to find you. You're safe as long as you stay in your room here. He reached your village."

Eve: "My family!" she said suddenly.

God: "They're safe! Now get some rest and wait for a message from Adam."

Adam had written his poem for Eve...he chose:

My heart is longing
My soul is yearning
To seek and find
A love so true
A soul divine

I believe in destiny
I believe in fate
I believe in one love
And the union of soul mates

Marsha Green

My life has been an endless search
Of someone just like you
My desire overwhelms me
I hunger just for you

CHAPTER 26

A DAY OF PREPARATION:

Thirty minutes later a cold gust of air entered the room and Roberson knew it was announcing the Devil. Drake Roberson was anxious to talk to the Devil with several questions in mind.

Devil: "Sing a song of sixpence, pocket full of rye."

Roberson: "Present."

Devil: "There were 10 and 20 black birds baked in a pie. Shoot Roberson! You've got questions and I've got answers."

Roberson: "What determines the winner?"

Devil: "It depends on how many shots you can take at him."

Roberson: "Will misses count against me?"

Devil: "The maid was in the kitchen making bread and honey, the king was in his parlor counting out his money. You shouldn't miss."

Roberson: "What type of rules are we going by?"

Devil: "Anything goes. Use that imagination of yours. Dust if off first."

Roberson: "What if he wins?" he asked exasperated.

Devil: "You know the score. You can't afford to lose, you'll enter purgatory."

Roberson was anxious.

Devil: "You're a real jabberwocky, my boy, nervous as a cat on a hot tin roof."

Roberson: "Jabberwocky?"

Devil: "Loquacious, talkative. Strategize, make your first move and plan some in your mind."

Roberson: "Right."

Devil: "You don't need a pep talk do you? Get with the program; it could cost you a year in purgatory. You'll pay for every sin you ever committed or even thought about. Meanwhile I go home the loser."

Roberson: "What is Reed planning?"

Devil: "Now you know my rules, my man, what are you anyways, Chicken Little bitching because the sky is falling?"

"Listen carefully," the Devil hissed, "Don't think about what you've got at stake; concentrate, focus, plan each move. The rest is trivial for now. You have no more questions," the devil said matter-of-factly…"Roger out."

Eve had just finished her messages from Drake and Adam. God had told her Dawn was alright and her people were safe from Morris and his gang. She would await word about the outcome of the psychic war. She lay down and closed her eyes. So Adam is actually Jay Reed, a famous movie star.

In Africa she had paid little attention to movies,

rarely going to them, but she knew of him. He was quite a "ladies man", a playboy. It was hard to believe that some 3,000 years ago they had been man and wife. She would have to get to know him all over again, she mused.

She also knew of Drake Roberson. He also had a big name. What she learned from God was that he was some kind of gangster and had possibly even sent hit men to kill people. She was nervous, but God had told her he had a plan in case there was a tie in the psychic war, or if Adam lost. There would be another way. God would play chess with the Devil for Eve.

CHAPTER 27

God decided to get Adam ready for the war ahead by sparring with him as in the old days, similar to the Greek Spartans and even in the days of Vietnam.

God entered Adam's hotel room. He was sitting by a table in the room anxiously smoking a cigarette.

God: "Get ready for a preview of what you're up against, Reed."

Adam snuffed out his butt and stood up.

God: "Sit on the floor with your back against the wall," he ordered.

God then introduced a visual of Drake Roberson in his mind.

Adam focused on the visual.

God: "I'll start now," he said.

With Roberson's visual, God produced a gun in his hand and began shooting bullets.

Adam was quick to dodge each one of them.

Adam then produced a knife in his mind and threw

it at Roberson aiming for his heart and missing it. Instead of hitting the target he hit Roberson in the middle of the chest.

God at that point produced a knife for Roberson and stabbed Adam in the stomach.

Adam went down and wrapped his arms around his torso.

God: "Expect the unexpected and plan moves on him," he instructed. "Always have a move in mind and watch him constantly. Focus, concentrate on Roberson. Watch his hands and respond with quick reflexes. Always keep in mind anything goes. He can copy you if you find a niche. Both of you are equal with deciding on which weapons to use. Booby traps may work sometimes where weapons fail."

God sparred with Adam for a few more moves, and then left him to rest.

Both men were ordered to go to bed at 9pm. God was the wakeup call at 6am. Adam had thought a lot about what he would do; and Roberson had strategized also. They both seemed ready. Adam slept fitfully. Roberson slept like a log.

CHAPTER 28

At precisely 6am God entered Adam's room and said, "Order room service, a light breakfast. There will be a jeep with a guide outside the hotel." Adam ordered toast and black coffee and ate slowly and methodically. He put on his jeans and a t-shirt, and then went through the lobby to find a jeep marked "Nature's Way" on the side of it. Eve's jeep for her tours he thought.

He got in and the jeep started up and headed south. Forty-five minutes later they were deep in the jungle of Kenya. God was already there. He motioned to a tree and said, "Sit up against it." Adam did as he was told.

Fifteen minutes later another jeep with "Nature's Way" on the side arrived and Adam spotted Drake Roberson riding in the back. He quickly stepped out of the jeep and Adam saw that he was wearing camouflage pants and a white t-shirt.

Roberson then bowed his head as if receiving instructions and sat up against a tree five feet from Adam.

The Devil entered Roberson's mind and told him to be ready for action and then just for fun began whistling the melody of the Star Spangled Banner.

God spoke then... "I'm opening your minds now. Can you see a visual of each other?"

Adam nodded and Roberson did the same. He could see clearly a visual of Drake Roberson standing up.

God then instructed "At the count of five begin: One... two... three... four... five!"

At the count of five, Drake Roberson pulled a pistol out of his pocket and began firing. Adam's visual fell flat on the ground. Adam then stood up and produced a machine gun and fired at Roberson's visual in his mind. Roberson's visual fell to the ground. Adam kept firing.

In the course of five seconds Roberson's visual threw a grenade at Adam. Roberson's visual then stood up to get a better look at his opponent, and Adam then hurled an axe through the air which hit Roberson in the chest.

Roberson went down. Then Roberson copied him and threw an axe barely missing Adam's head.

Adam tried to distract him by starting the Lord's Prayer. "Our Father who art in Heaven." he said.

Adam then fired a gun at Roberson's head and missed him.

Roberson bent down to dodge the bullet.

"Hallowed be thy name."

Adam threw a knife and hit Roberson square in the chest. "Thy kingdom come, thy will be done... "
Roberson fell to the ground.

Adam threw an axe and hit Roberson in the head. Roberson pulled himself up off the ground in Adam's mind and threw another grenade at him. His aim was off from where the axe had hit his head.

Adam began distracting him by reciting the 23rd Psalm. "Yea though I walk through the valley of the shadow of death, I will fear no evil, for thou art with me."

Suddenly as a distraction for Adam, Roberson's mind produced a circle of snakes around him.

One snake had reached Adam and was crawling up his leg. It was a large rattlesnake and was in the position to strike him. Adam's visual reached for the snake, grabbed it, and threw it to the side of him. Before long Roberson produced three other snakes and coiled one around Adam's neck while the other two were slithering around his ankles.

At that precise moment Adam said loudly "Thy rod and thy staff, they comfort me" and then his visual produced a can of gasoline and poured it over Roberson's visual.

He then produced a book of matches.

As Adam was attempting to light a match, Roberson's snake struck him and his visual winced at the bite. Adam's visual was paralyzed by the venom. Adam regained his composure a minute later and by then Roberson had produced a rocket launcher. He fired it at Adam's heart.

Adam produced a shield a split second before that and placed it across his chest. Then by sheer will power Adam focused on Roberson's neck, twisted it around, and broke it. Adam gasped at the sight when he saw Roberson's head had been completely turned around. Roberson's visual was completely still and lying on the ground.

Mother Nature drew a sharp intake of breath and the Devil's jaw dropped. Regaining his composure the Devil exclaimed "Egad" and Mother Nature's eyes rolled towards the Heavens. There was silence for about fifteen seconds and then God entered his mind.

"It's all over Adam, you're the champion now. Get back to the hotel." Adam blinked and looked over to see Roberson rubbing the back of his neck. Adam was exhausted. He sat up against the tree and closed his eyes. When he opened them he was alone in the jungle with the exception of the guide who was waiting in the jeep for him. He finally arose and headed for the vehicle.

CHAPTER 29

Roberson rode in the back of the jeep in silence. He was stunned by the fact Reed had won so quickly and with precision had twisted and broken his neck in the psychic war. He was in a daze, bewildered, and dumbfounded. Hairs stood up on the back of his neck when the visual of the Devil entered his mind. The visual was of a dark shadow, with red horns and wings, and two black eyes. There were yellow slits in those coal black eyes. It was a hideous face.

"Drat!" the Devil hissed. He was melancholy.

Roberson: "Present." he said, and then he swallowed. He had a sense of foreboding.

Devil: "Hell's bells" he sang.

Roberson: "What happens now?"

The devil gave a low chuckle, and then cackled.

Devil: Here's a riddle for you, Roberson. What's red and white and walked all over?"

Roberson winced, panic-stricken and confused he replied "Don't know."

Devil: "It's your cane you'll use upon your return to Earth, a blind man!"

Roberson was terrified and aghast at what he comprehended.

The devil began singing "The sweetest dreams I've ever had… were when I went completely mad."

Roberson felt a rush of cold air around him and broke out into a sweat.

Devil: "You were doomed from the beginning, Roberson. I'm a poet now."

Roberson pushed his mother to an early grave.

His soul goes to the Devil.

His soul he cannot save.

He broke his nanny's neck.

He's now a nervous wreck.

He shot his father in cold blood.

Now his name is in the mud.

The Devil laughed amusedly, "Ah."

Devil: "You'll return to Earth," the Devil lit a cigarette, "in about a year, Roberson," then he took a long drag, "The Grim Reaper sees you on your death bed. Oh! There's one more thing. Roberson was in the parlor counting out his money. Money makes the world go round."

The Devil laughed, and then continued, "Your money, all of it, goes to preventing animal abuse and neglect. Now go home with your tail between your legs, you loathsome worthless prick." The Devil was gone.

CHAPTER 30

Back at the hotel Adam took a hot shower and ordered a light lunch of tuna fish salad, fries and coke. God entered the room and motioned towards the bed. "Get some shut eye," he instructed Adam. He fell into the bed and went to sleep.

When he awakened it was dark. He looked over at the clock on his nightstand and saw that it was near midnight. He fell back into a deep sleep.

At 6am God entered his room and gave him further instructions. He was on another mission. He left the hotel in a rented jeep and headed south again into the jungle of Kenya.

For an hour and a half Adam waited in the jungle for Eve. Her jeep arrived 30 minutes later. As she stepped out of the vehicle, she could see Adam in the distance holding onto a newborn giraffe. He was grinning at her and caressing the baby giraffe.

"Yes!" she exclaimed and ran to him. For the next

hour they watched as Dawn, the mother giraffe cared for her newborn.

They talked for hours about his life as an actor, of not finding anyone to have a relationship with, about her life of abuse and neglect by her parents, of her family of natives that she lived with since the age of 20. They spoke to each other briefly about what happened in the Garden of Eden. After an awkward moment of silence, Adam then reached over and kissed her passionately.

God watched over them and was pleased.

CHAPTER 31

Three hours later, deep in the jungles of Africa, Adam and Eve stood face to face.

Eve's animals were also present. In a tree nearby a family of chimpanzees sat on branches and a herd of zebras were in the distance. Dawn and her newborn giraffe sat beside her.

God entered the jungle and said to them "You and Eve are now married in the eyes of God. You may kiss the bride."

Adam and Eve shared a long, affectionate kiss and Adam gently held her close.

God observed that it was a perfect wedding day for them.

Eve took Adam on a tour of the jungle. She had hand signals to the monkeys in the trees and they followed them everywhere yakking happily. She approached a herd of zebras and spent time petting them and talking in a soothing tone. Then they walked a mile deeper into the jungle and came upon a den of lions.

Adam was tense as he witnessed the lion looking at them in a lazy fashion.

From the den emerged a lioness that came forward to greet Eve.

She caressed the lioness' head and then the big cat rolled her over onto the ground and started wrestling with her. They rolled from side to side and it seemed the lioness always took a precaution in laying right on her because of the weight she held.

Adam marveled at the sight. He was completely entranced.

They were alone in the jungle and stood face to face. Adam took Eve in his arms and kissed her ardently. His hands were shaking in excitement as he took off her t-shirt and then slowly unzipped her jeans. She stepped out of them and was before Adam naked. He drew in a sharp intake of breath in wonderment of her exquisite body.

Eve's breasts were full with gorgeous pink nipples, a small waistline, and narrow hips. He looked into her large blue eyes and then took off his shirt and jeans. He reached out to her and embraced her again and began kissing her with a hunger he had never experienced before.

Cupping her breasts momentarily he ran his hands down her body. With his hand he touched her vagina and was surprised to find her warm and already moist from the excitement of kissing him.

She moaned with pleasure.

Adam then guided her to the ground. Eve again moaned with pleasure as he made hard and fast thrusts inside of her. He held her tightly and together they came with an explosion of passion. Following this he lay aside her kissing her face and neck.

So this is what I've been missing all my life he thought and smiled inwardly.

An hour later God entered their minds and spoke. "Now listen carefully, Mother Nature goes away forever. She is forbidden to ever play tricks on mankind again. She will not be responsible for the creation of new mental illnesses or birth defects. She will put her mind to use by creating a new species of animals. Her extinct animals may be saved by a new procedure of cloning. She cannot observe the two of you in Heaven and will never see you again. She has been officially retired from evil deeds. You're forever safe from her Adam, she was completely stupefied at the outcome of the psychic war when you broke Roberson's neck, splendid job."

Adam smiled. GOD continued, "Drew Morris and his crew were apprehended at Eve's village by police authorities after Eve alerted them with a phone call during the psychic war. They were taken into custody by a huge gang of policemen, taken to jail, and are now awaiting a court date to be set. Eve, you will be testifying against them.

"Yes!" she exclaimed.

God continued, "Drake Roberson will donate all of his money to stopping animal abuse and neglect and will live on welfare the rest of his life. His soul will enter purgatory for a year or so and then will return to Earth. He will be punished for all his evil deeds.

Now at the time of your deaths your souls will be automatically sent to Heaven. You'll be transformed to the Divine State in that Heaven and meet again when Eve reaches the age of 20."

God went on, "Meanwhile I am planning the Second Coming with Jesus Christ".

"When is the Second Coming?" Adam asked.

"It's projected for approximately 50 years from now, The Devil comes back with a new Anti-Christ and my Son will be in a battle with him. Right at this very moment the Devil is licking his wounds. He's challenging me to a chess match; just for fun." God said offhandedly.

"How do you play?" Adam asked.

"We keep a Chess board in our minds with all the pieces". God answered.

"Wow!" Adam said and whistled softly.

God: "He loves the thrill of playing, but I haven't lost a match yet! Now, be good to yourselves. I'll be with you at your deaths."

And with that God was gone. Adam and Eve stood alone again.

Adam smiled down at her and kissed her on the nose.

CHAPTER 32

Devil: "Drat!"

God chuckled.

Devil: "They're probably naked as jaybirds now and fornicating."

God: "You're mad as a hatter, Devil."

Devil: "What do you mean by that?"

God: "Demented."

Devil: "There is more than one way to skin a cat."

God: "It's over. Adam won fair and square."

Devil: "Roberson's mind is now at a point of no return. He's a paper tiger."

God: "Speak English now."

Devil: "He's something less tough or menacing than he appears now," he explained.

God: "What do you have in the works now?"

Devil, lighting up a cigarette and taking a slow drag: "Looking for a new Anti-Christ. Roberson always rubbed me the wrong way anyway. He's now afraid of his own shadow."

God: "I'm preparing Jesus Christ for the final battle."

Devil: "The show must go on!"

God: "Mother Nature said the very same thing".

Devil: "Ya know she wore the pants in the family 25 lifetimes. How is the old wind bag doing now?"

God: "Docile and meek as a lamb."

Devil: (snuffs out his cigarette on his leg) "Hey, how about playing a mean game of chess? Then I'm here today and gone tomorrow."

The Devil wheezes and laughs at his own joke.

God: "You're on!"

A chessboard materializes between them.

GOD: (Lights up a cigar) "Make the first move Devil."